David J. [illegible]
October 23, 1975
Lenox, Mass.

Any Day of Your Life

Any Day of Your Life

BY DAVID KHERDIAN

THE OVERLOOK PRESS, *Woodstock, New York*
THE BOOKSTORE PRESS, *Lenox, Massachusetts*

Grateful acknowledgement is made to the editors
and publishers who first published many of these
poems as broadsides, and in periodicals and
anthologies: The University of Connecticut, The
Bellevue Press, Arts Extension Service of Continuing
Education, University of Massachusetts, Arts
Action Press, Literary Tabloid, Workshop, Canto,
The DeKalb Literary Arts Journal, The Margarine
Maypole Orangoutang Express, riverrun, Schist,
Poetry Now, Hudson Review Anthology, Community
of Friends, The Second Berkshire Anthology,
Out of Sight; A Primer of Domestic Poetry,
and Armenian-North American Poets: An Anthology.

Published in 1975 by
The Overlook Press
Lewis Hollow Road
Woodstock, N.Y. 12498
and
The Bookstore Press
9 Housatonic Street
Lenox, Massachusetts 01240
Copyright © 1975 by David Kherdian
All Rights Reserved. No part of this
publication may be reproduced or transmitted
in any form or by any means, electronic or
mechanical, including photocopy, recording,
or any information or storage and retrieval
system now known or to be invented,
without permission in writing from the
publisher, except by a reviewer who wishes to
quote brief passages in connection with a
review written for inclusion in a magazine,
newspaper or broadcast.
ISBN: 0-87951-034-X
Library of Congress Catalog Card Number:
75-4381
Printed in the United States by The Studley Press, Inc.

Books of Poetry by David Kherdian

ON THE DEATH OF MY FATHER AND OTHER POEMS
HOMAGE TO ADANA
LOOKING OVER HILLS
A DAVID KHERDIAN SAMPLER
THE NONNY POEMS
ANY DAY OF YOUR LIFE

CONTENTS

I

Re-Making the Muse
20:XII:72
Starting Out
While You Were Out Shopping I Started
   This Poem for Book V
Cat Time
Re-Entry: 7 January 1973
Entry 19:XI:73
Opening the Door on the 18th of January,
   Late in the Evening, To Let the Cat In
Cat & Wife
1973, the 10th of April, 4 Inches of Snow
Reading a Book, etc.
Alone
On the Steps
The Contest
More of the Same
4:I:74
The Jump Up & Write Down 15th of April Poem
Almost
22:IV:73
Anniversary Song
2:VIII:73
From the Window
16:IV:73
In the Tradition
Me and the Chickadee
A Letter from the Muse
26:VIII:73
A Poem for the Cats
Onions from New Hampshire

II

Mulberry Trees
Remembering Mihran
Lyme, New Hampshire
14:X:74
Pigeons
Calling My Name
The Toy Soldier
When Form Answers Urge and Follows
Leaves are Tree Shadows
Summer's End
Her
For all the Female Chauvinist Lambs
The Fast
While *Brubeck Plays Brubeck*
Endlessly the Poem
For a Poet
While Reading the *American Poetry Review*
Again

For Nonny

I

RE-MAKING THE MUSE

You take two cats,
one squirming for love
beside the woman drinking
sherry on the couch,
across from the man
writing these lines—
and you have this poem.

Add quiet
add late evening,
say it is early autumn
and the man has not
written a poem in months.

Say all this
and be grateful for
what came before
and for what will
come in time.

20:XII:72

stillness
snowfall
in the valley
across the mountain
a bird flies
in the cathedral
of the wind

STARTING OUT

the crouch   the wiggle
slowly slowly slowly
swiftly the sprung leap
into forgetfulness
the absent look   the
sidelong glance at nothing
and the mad backward two-step
into a new game of feisty

WHILE YOU WERE OUT SHOPPING
I STARTED THIS POEM FOR BOOK V

the plants are breathing
in your room
wandering through
wondering what next to do
I clear my throat
for the perched birds
to hear
and begin my speech

CAT TIME

Missak has had the day's adventure
Sumpat, the wild cat before, long disappeared;

returned, entered and ate his food.
But not without raised backhair and snarl.

A cat's war with the kingdom or life.
But quickly afterwards he lounges on

the couch, forepaw hanging off, gets
set to sleep and tumbles down.

RE-ENTRY: 7 JANUARY 1973

Nonny, in her diary, avoids
the keeping of what is said,

the motions there giving hint
only to the movements here.

If I say, Waiting is not my
long suit, and she replies,

Wait a fucking minute, who
would know, if thus recorded,

what the question, who replied.
Is the answer, she got up to

make the popcorn? Chances are
the diary neglects to say.

ENTRY 19:XI:73

Phallic symbols, candles,
my wife says, excusing
her taste for their smell—
laboring, it seems to me
at carefully feeding the
drippings to molten wax,
sighing—well, orgiastically,
or so I say in the face
of her passionate defense—
and so, bored, amused, be-
mused, dissatisfied, or just
lovingly defenseless and
defending, we rest, wrestle,
cease to resist and enjoy
our drink, candle, late
night talk-down fistless
fight fast tomfoolery,
get up and go to bed.

OPENING THE DOOR ON THE 18TH OF JANUARY, LATE IN THE EVENING, TO LET THE CAT IN

as the moon glides thru
streaking clouds

the cat with frightened
tail

sniffs & enters
his only home

CAT & WIFE

Holding the basket on your lap
you shake a packet of
Burpee seeds, while I answer
from across the room—
"an audience of one,"
for Missak has moved from
my chair to yours,
involved now in this
new noise and play,
as you ready spring
in midwinter,
summer plans in your head,
winter out the door.

1973, THE 10TH OF APRIL, 4 INCHES OF SNOW

Constipated all day,
mewing in his sleep,
with sidelong angry
glances when awake,
the springtime cat sits
at the window
and watches it fall.

But forced outside for
the country walk
to the mailbox, he
warms to the cold
& romps (knows he's
pretty: black body
on white snow,
that falls & grows
at his traveling
feet), but alarmed
momentarily by the
invisible cow across
the long meadow, mooing
her own discontent,
and startled by dog barks
& the neighbor's coaxing call.

Then he turns with us with
the morning mail to hear:
"Thata boy, thata boy"—
Barbara's booming voice:
her dog has obeyed—
and now we are home,
looking out the window again,
happy & refreshed (the day's
mild adventure), while
silently again, outside,
it falls and falls.

READING A BOOK, ETC.

reading a book
late at night
mid-winter
waiting for spring
to arrive
I glance up at Nonny
& begin to picture
us in our summer
garden—
seed catalogs
on the floor,
fire burning hotly
in the grate—
and I push our growing
age against
those spring green
garden thoughts
& know that our
eternal moment
is not now
but then
not writing this
furiously waiting
but seed & shovel
in hand
greeting the
new earth
our final comfort
and friend

ALONE

staring at
the empty shoes,
one cocked
over the other
below the
sleeping cat—
I look up:
she's not here
but in the kitchen
making bread
in stocking
feet

ON THE STEPS

This is the hour for poets
and cats
Missak purring curled on
my lap
Nonny drawing on the next
room table
outside the green pine
brown trees of winter
hold in their lanes
the puckered sweetly hanging
apples
the deer will come and find

THE CONTEST

You are drawing the great
fantasy childhood book
neither of us ever saw,
from out of our own early
wandering-wondering-imaginations;
beautiful, sensual colors;
robes, ouds & dumbegs,
mixed with the flowing
action of robbers & rewards,
none of it real, all of it
more than real; a woman,
two lovers (both bandits)
ignorant of her double life;
horses, jezvehs, samovars & camels,
choruses of colors; and through
it all the children within us
dancing with wide-eyed dazed
amazement and regard.

MORE OF THE SAME

Nonny, with her seeds to
seedling book on her lap,
sits in her chair of knowing,
looks up provocatively,
clasps her hands behind
her head
& gives me pointers
on how all of it
is to be done—
come summer, come
garden time,
when the literary organic
growing lessons
become reality
& we move out of the
comfortable chambers
of learning
& back into the sunshine
of growth & coming life.

4:I:74

Writing on the tear sheet
of the local health food store—
a poem of quiet to the fireplace;
the cat on the bed, my wife at
the window; while snow and the
dust of time surrounds the
neighborhood and our lives.

THE JUMP UP & WRITE DOWN 15TH OF APRIL POEM

And so, here comes Nonny
talking into the room,
sits down & keeps going,
so & so and such & such;
while outside Missak is
chasing a hornet the
spring weather has released
into the morning air. And
as always in the early day,
I sit drugged, waiting also
to bloom—and poems such as
this come to mind & go out
of mine (seldom put to paper),
and there are other things:
a star review in Virginia
Kirkus, worry over taxes,
royalties have slipped this
quarter on one of Nonny's
books, the folks in Englewood
are happy and confused—
it's fairly endless, not
to mention curious,
but when the sun is shining
as it is today, you know it is
all going to melt away with
the heat of it—hot, sunny
& quiet, which is just about
all we want (and now I'm off
thinking about childhood)
during the early spring season,
calendar 1973, any day of
your life.

ALMOST

the woodpecker
hammers
on the
lilac bush
out for
branch lice
gnats & goodies
at the end
of winter
beside the
abandoned feeder:
the soft colors
of spring
in the air
and on the way

22:IV:73

A touch of yellow mixed
with green, a hint of
purple below red-brown
bursting buds of leaves
against the grey black
bark of forest trees—
and in the distance, slowly
across the land, the sound
of many birds, just arrived,
calling, crying, throwing
their voices against the
sky, against the land.

ANNIVERSARY SONG

We have worked too hard, and
strained too hard to live this life—
illness has grown out of our
strength—to persist has sometimes
taxed our will to go on.

Now, having given over to our age,
our frailty and the coming tide
(still yet the years will swell)
we return again to the unfolding hour
to make again each act of art, our
talk, the quiet walk in the dark—
the moon—and the fixed hours of rise
and movement and rest.

Thus it has happened we arrive
again and again to each other
with two years added to our
brows, and bow without moving
to our life.

2:VIII:73

rain on the window
cats asleep on the couch
you in a faraway room
my silent eye
in the changing light

FROM THE WINDOW

There is something beautiful
out there beyond the window
beyond the growing lawn—
Nonny walking, brooding,
thru the yard, returning
her thoughts to the earth
and bringing to my own mind
the fruits of another summer
garden—on the blazing tips
of another summer sun—
and Missak frolicking & dancing
at her hesitant heel . . .
the three winds of the family
with all elements in moving
conjunction, caught in a drama
only I can see . . . and we are
all atmosphere . . . I, shimmering
at the window (dazed by love),
watching Nonny kneeling on the
new sod—and Missak, suddenly
still, turns & looks beyond,
beyond grass & woods & home,
attuned to his other secret life.

16:IV:73

Missak on his
rocktop moss
covered throne
(in our fern &
flower garden)
sits & catches
flies and keeps
his belly warm

IN THE TRADITION

My family, my wife says,
is all that is important
to me, and saying that
she turns and gives her
full attention to the toll—
house cookies that will soon
emerge from the batter
being beaten by the mixer
that frightens the cat.

And so, the three of us are
in the kitchen, 11:15 P.M.—
a late night drink for me,
a mild fright for the cat,
and cookies for my wife.

Family enough or not, this
is who we are, where we live
and how it is done. It is
part of the formula of life,
and keeping it good and simple
in a poem helps to give pre-
eminence to life. Give thanks
to my wife.

ME AND THE CHICKADEE

two birds on the bird-feeder
side by side
with a 3rd above,
now one jumps in the
belly feeder
& the other two
are gone
and another arrives—
still another—and another—
now all but one are gone (again)
and he, belly deep in the wooden
feeder,
is throwing seeds up and out
as he sinks deeper into
what he knows and is
and is his life

inside the window
I am done with
lunch, growing fat
on cookies, washing
them down with
tea:
we are different
creatures, the similarities
between us tenuous
at best,
but we are quaintly
attached to this place
where we spend
our days that
are going by
and similarly fat
with life

A LETTER FROM THE MUSE

After a long heat steaming
from damp earth morning,
that followed a night of
intermittent rain—along
comes an afternoon breeze
to blow it all away.

Too hot to move in the morning,
too rested to care by afternoon,
I sit and wait for the cat to
know I am ready—

comes and sits on my lap and
purrs me this poem.

26:VIII:73

the grasshopper
that leapt into the
snow-on-the-mountain
chased the white
moth out

A POEM FOR THE CATS

If I talk sweetly to Anoush
she immediately purrs, moves
her head to one side & asks
to be loved—while Missak
across the porch
rolls over seductively & says,
with his one cat sound:
do it too to me.

ONIONS FROM NEW HAMPSHIRE

Nonny, in her beets
and celery garden—
gone to seed to woodchuck
to rain and bugs—
brings in her only harvest,
immature but bone-white
immaculate onions
with gangly green stems,
and asks that I bend
to her will and theirs
and bind them top and bottom
in plastic bags—
to carry to our new home;
their tears our only sorrow,
their food our only salvage
from the droopy dog days
of this summer gone.

II

MULBERRY TREES

When
as a small boy
I saw them ripen against
the early summer sun
I stopped alone for an hour
and ate until my fingers
took an ancient purple stain

until something remembered
a smaller, knotty tree
in a barren, rocky landscape
before an older, quieter sun

and I went home a little
sadder, a little gladdened
and standing on the porch
my mother and father
saw their Armenian son.

REMEMBERING MIHRAN

the log that
fell off the grate
caused another to
slip into the pocket
left by its place,
and suddenly the
fire leapt into
bursting flame—

and I was in your
living room
years ago
warmed   not by the
fire   but by your
intelligence
poking the logs
humming under
your breath
turning and
cursing the night
in Armenian

LYME, NEW HAMPSHIRE

the flea-bitten dog
in front of the
ramshackle garage
in the aging New
England village
(on the last day
of March)

sits alone in the
new dust of spring

14:X:74

The dry log fire in
the open fireplace
is writing an old message
on the brain of the
transfixed kitten,
while beside her momma cat
curls for back warmth
and sleeps,
already knowing what
she does not know
and doesn't care to know.

PIGEONS

Because we have cut down
the dying elm tree
where they cooed
they fly higher
travel in fewer numbers
glide in the blue sky
less afraid
closer to the great thunderer
their god.

CALLING MY NAME

Remember when
Superior Street
held the world
swaying in its arms
wafting innocence
for miles
down that block
elm trees and fences
to carve & kiss behind

brother of many names
sisters in the night
come now and add your
incense to the hour
while I sing of a lost
child's fireflies.

THE TOY SOLDIER

A toy like the one I played with as a child
is in the antique shop down the street—
the brown soldier, arm still poised,
handgrenade in hand . . .

He never threw it . . . the game went on . . .
I kept him in a box with others . . .
and shared my game with friends.

Such friends they were, my toys, so
trusting was I of the fun, but now
I cannot take this soldier home again
(my own soldiers lost and gone) . . .

Only $3 says the tag that dangles from his head
but I fear his poised arm has already fallen
and our gentle hearts are dead.

WHEN FORM ANSWERS URGE AND FOLLOWS

the word unleashed
tracks a poem across
the heart—
my wife murmuring
in the other room
sets in motion the
tremor that swells
to language—
though in another form,
it is an only answer—
the anguished excitement
of what leaps for
catching what
defies—

LEAVES ARE TREE SHADOWS

As leaves grace the
air with their sweep
and silent fall,
the cat steps
from the curb—
knows without turning
no cars will come,
and enters this half
of the world

were the rain
continues to fall
and dead leaves
are refacing time—
tree shadows that
come and go

SUMMER'S END

On days such as this
when the spent rain of early fall
drips from pine needles
above the rain-covered ground

When jays and squirrels
are the only movement
above the blanket that descends
to muffle every living sound

It is then we are called
from our homes to stand as sentries,
anonymous at last,
no more than a block of solid quiet
in the liquid quiet night.

HER

Late at night on our block
down from my house
on the way to my friend's—
black black the sky,
the white moon on her house
in the faraway night.

FOR ALL THE FEMALE CHAUVINIST LAMBS

Hi

THE FAST

Trying to discipline myself
  to eat less,
a moral lesson I'm badly
      in need of—
I savor the *rojik* my mother
has sent all the way from
  California

            western walnuts
            coated in a shell
            of jellied grape
            juice & rolled in
            a coating of pow-
            dered sugar

an Armenian delicacy from which
    deliverence
         is not easy/
and so
    then,
        the first small bite is
easy
    but the restraint sends an
avalanche of saliva
           down
and drops a message on the head
    of my animal
which has suddenly opened
      my mouth
    (making a sound I notice)
and before I can get my *rojik*
    out of the way
        it lunges   and
bites my hand with my teeth

WHILE *Brubeck Plays Brubeck*

I always wanted to write
a poem while Brubeck played
Brubeck—

something in his
walking blues
that carried all
meaning
down the empty
streets of
forgotten time,

for here we are,
1974,
& only the recording
and I are left
in the shades
& shadows
of what the remembrance
of his work regains—

telling us only
that tenderness
endures.

ENDLESSLY THE POEM

To change the skin of one's poetry,
like the line I have marked with
my pen—dividing this poem on the page
from the one above—is like a curve,
a melody caught in the middle of life,
and I remember my youth for a moment
as a sun-arc dream-circle that has ended—
for now as I come to the age of forty
and move beyond, I come also to blunted
lines that end each day at the top of
the stairs, at the foot of the bed,
where I stand for a moment before
lying down. These are the beginning
years of the end of my life, the infancy
of old age: the first 40 just ended,
the next 40 just begun.

FOR A POET

I wish I could say
to you, my friend,
drop everything
you're thinking
come out of your
skin alive
and dance
with me breathless
and heartless . . .
we have our wives
we too, oh . . .
life's a torture
we can leave alone.

WHILE READING *The American Poetry Review*

The call of the Bobwhite
breaks the sudden night.
I turn from the paper and
wait to have it call again—
ah! the second and only
poems I've had tonight.

AGAIN

The act of writing, after
long silence, is benediction.
To hold the pen in hand, to
fill a white page with
scratches of black ink,
is to be in tune again
with the mysteries
and to be in the service of
others who have written and
will write. "Genius is hard
work," I say aloud, and write
it down, ending this poem
only to begin the next.

DAVID KHERDIAN was born in Racine, Wisconsin in 1931. After graduating from the University of Wisconsin in 1960, he moved to California, where, for more than ten years, he divided his time between Fresno and San Francisco. In 1966 he founded The Giligia Press, which introduced new poetry to readers and poets across the country. He married artist-illustrator, Nonny Hogrogian in 1971, their courtship and marriage being chronicled in THE NONNY POEMS. The first section of ANY DAY OF YOUR LIFE continues that chronicle, from their first home in New Hampshire to their present one in upstate New York where they now live on a small farm.